PICKLES
THE
PIDDLIN' PUP

KIMBERLY WALKER   **GEORGE SWEETLAND**

Printed in the United States of America
First Printing, 2021
Hardcover: ISBN 978-1-7357621-1-1
Paperback: ISBN 978-1-7357621-2-8

Edited by: Racquel Henry
Illustrations and cover art by: George Sweetland
Layout by: Travis D. Peterson

www.KimWalkerAuthor.com

PICKLES
THE
PIDDLIN'
PUP

OH NO!

KIMBERLY WALKER   GEORGE SWEETLAND

Pickles piddles on the run.

Pickles piddles in the sun.

Mama Myrie shouts, "No Pickles! No!"
Pickles squats on the couch. She is ready to go.

Pickles piddles where others wouldn't.

Pickles piddles where she shouldn't.

DON'T YOU DARE!

Pickles piddles on the floor.

"Not another piddling drop," Mama Tita tells her.

"Please, no more!"

CAUTION

WET FLOOR

Nowhere is safe, not the tiniest nook.

Pickles is crafty. She piddled
where you are touching this book.

Pickles prances to the door. Pickles piddles on the floor.

Her mamas try to teach the proper way.

"You must piddle outside, Pickles," they both say.

She doesn't listen. She ruffs and huffs looking for something else to christen.

Pickles piddles on Mama Tita

"That's it," shouts Mama Myrie!
"I am consulting Siri!"

"You want to know how to fix a piddling pup? Let me help you look that up..."

"Puppy training pads," reads Mamma Tita aloud.

"Let's save that idea to the cloud."

Mama Myrie and Mama Tita load a tail wagging Pickles into the car. Pickles thinks we are going to the toy store, oh yes we are.

No toys are purchased. Not a single one. This cannot be happening, thinks Pickles. This is no fun.

Pickles piddles when they get home.

She piddles outside, but on the front porch gnome.

A piddle pad is placed next to the doggy door.

Pickles sniffs the pad like she is bored.

PUPPY PIDDLE PADS

She slides on it with her rump.

She is going to do it! She is going to squat in the right place
and take a...DUMP!

Mama Tita sighs.

Mama Marie screams!

Pickles picks up the poopy piddle pad.

Ruff! Huff! Her mamas have had enough of her schemes!

Pickles runs past her mommas in a whoosh of brown speckled white! They zig left and she zags right!

Pickles screeches to a stop.

She drops the pad with a plop.

Pickles piddles on her favorite toy.

"Ruh roh," she barks.

Piddling for once did not spark joy.

It stinks. It stunk! Pickles cannot believe her
piddling smells like a skunk!

Her mamas catch up to her, ready to scold. As Mama Myrie lifts a pointed finger, Pickles does as she has over and over been told.

Pickles romps and runs between Mama Myrie and Mama Tita.
She zooms fast like a cheetah.

Pickles vrooms out the doggy door. She is outside to do more than explore.

Pickles piddles in the grass. She is sorry for her giving her mamas so much sass.

Mama. Myrie and Mama Tita give Pickles a hug and a kiss.
Pickles licks them back just like this.

Schloop. Lick. Slurp. She gets so excited she lets out a...

Pickles no longer piddles everywhere, instead,
she burps loud without a care.

CPSIA information can be obtained
at www.ICGtesting.com
Printed in the USA
LVRC091341191121
703840LV00003B/80